fuck away

fade away

A Novel by Austin Nguyen

www.BabypiePublishing.com

To shine a light when hope isn't seen

Acknowledgments

To my mom, who has loved and supported me every day in my life.

To my four closest friends, who make me feel like I belong in this world.

Part One

Note to Self

Chapter 1

I'm sorry.

I'm sorry I couldn't conform to the regular stereotype of being a guy. I apologize for my incapability to properly throw a football. I ask you to have mercy on my lack of pervertedness and guy friends. I sincerely regret not having the physique of the star quarterback on the football team in order to get a girlfriend. I hope you can forgive me for being all the things a guy wasn't supposed to be: for excelling at academics, for talking to girls, for playing with little kids instead of raging at my computer. I can see that you don't desire my existence in this world where traditional values and concepts are the only things that are accepted. Where falling behind on academics but being the fastest runner on the track team is tolerated and expected. Where screwing a crapload of girls is applauded but not dating even one is looked down upon. Where wearing a shirt of something you love means you're homosexual and, therefore, a lower part of society and deserve to get shit on. I'm sorry I've been breathing for fourteen years. Please forgive me for taking so much time to realize I'm unwanted.

I'll leave,

Michael

That's a pretty good draft, don't you think? I mean, it could probably use more comedy, but I don't know. Death is an extremely delicate subject and lightheartedness doesn't exactly go well with it.

Chapter 2

May 25, 2015

I couldn't breathe.

"You okay?" my best friend, Celine, asked.

I barely nodded.

"It's just one test; it's not the end of the world. I mean, this isn't gonna make or break . . ." She trailed off as she noticed I was getting more stressed out.

I hated it when people said that because what they really should be saying is it's not the end of *your* world. The world can continue without a lot of people; I mean, just look at the hundreds of deaths they show on TV. But the lives of certain people who relied on those who died in 9/11 or the terrorist attack on Nice—those lives will never be the same and their world as they know it ends. So, yeah, tests don't end *the* world, but they can ruin reputation, invite comments, and shatter *one person's* world.

I started shrinking; I bent over my desk, crossed my legs, and crossed my arms so that my left palm was touching my right elbow and vice versa. I attempted to take one deep, steady breath, but when I exhaled, the air came out shakily and I started to shiver.

"What's wrong with you?" the teacher, Miss Johns, asked while peering above her witch-like, wrinkled nose.

I looked up. Shit. She was gesturing toward me with her pruney hands, a result from her eighty-five years of life. Light started to gleam off Miss Johns' golden ring as she held out her left hand to point at me while the entire class fell to an eerie silence immediately.

"Nothing, I'm just a bit nervous about the test." There goes all the nonexistent confidence people thought I had.

"Well, then, maybe you should've dropped honors," she said, while her broom of white hair moved when she flipped the stack of tests over.

What the fuck? Was it legal to say that to a student? How hasn't this teacher gotten fired yet?

I gulped as I shifted my attention back to my desk.

"Do you need to be excused to the office to go see the counselor about a schedule change?"

I focused my gaze on my lap through the long bangs of my short black hair as the teacher continued and tension built.

"If it's too much pressure, just leave. You can do it right now if you want or after sixth period."

I considered standing up and walking out the door before I took another deep breath. I glanced at Miss Johns and the annoyed expression present in her swarthy face before she started calling out names. I kept my dark brown eyes glued to the floor and the front ends of my blue, worn-down sneakers when I had to stand up and take the test from her. When I was about to settle down in my chair, Miss Johns said, "I'd be happy to schedule an appointment with Mrs. Louvsa for you if you want to move to regular math."

I spent the next fifteen minutes silently as I corrected the five problems I missed on the test. I wondered how students from last year's class forgot to mention that Miss Johns was A TOTAL BIOTCH. I mean, they told me that she was mean and she tore up your homework if you worked on it during class, but they never told me she embarrassed students in front of the class by insulting their intelligence. That's not mean; that's being a douchebag. I stormed out of the classroom when the bell rang for sixth period. I was the first person out the door. I could feel the heat manifesting behind my eyes, but I pushed it back; breakdowns are for home, break ups are for school.

Chapter 3

"What happened in math class wasn't right for a teacher to say. You holding up?" Celine asked, pushing her curly blonde hair behind her ear to get a better glimpse of me.

The last thing I felt was *okay*, but as I looked into my best friend's almond-shaped, blue eyes, I saw that constant fragility from the first time we met in front of the library courtyard at the elementary school that warranted comforting.

"Fine," I said while smiling weakly, forcing my thin lips to form the slightest curve.

"Good, good," Celine responded, as the fragility I've grown familiar with for eight years vanished and was replaced with a bright, white smile.

I could tell she had a profound desire to ask me how I did on the test to act as a segue for her to tell me how she did; Celine was subtly self-centered like that, and I felt like the only person who realized that and accepted it is me. In order to distract her from the stress I probably caused her from that little skirmish in sixth period, I asked her how she did on the test, even though I was going through physical pain thinking about the word *math*. But knowing Celine for a while, I knew she was concerned about academics almost always. I'd gotten used to the self-inflicted pain that would come up when discussing grades and the way she'd became a masochist.

"What'd you get on the test?" I asked after sighing.

"Oh, my God!" she exclaimed with a wide smile across her face. I took a step back while covering my ears, afraid I was going to go deaf if I stood too close to her. "You won't believe it. All those problems I thought I got wrong, I got right. Like number four and number eight. I put symmetric property for both of those, but Elise said they were reflexive and I thought I would get marked down for those. But apparently . . . wait, no, I actually got those wrong. But . . . " She trailed off. I turned around, realizing I was the next person to answer the entry question so I could get into the classroom for Spanish.

"¿Cómo se dice *yellow* en Español?"

"Amarillo."

At least I could get one thing in my life right.

I stood right next to the door, waiting for Celine to go through so I could take a seat next to her. After she entered, we both walked to the counter to put our materials for math down and take our Spanish workbooks to our desks.

"How did you do on the math test?" Celine asked while settling in her seat, attempting to make small talk so we wouldn't sit awkwardly in silence.

"The usual C-plus." I said while slamming my workbook on the table and sighing.

"Hey, at least you did better than John. He got a D-plus and he's planning to drop in a week."

"Yeah, but John has other things he can be good at," I said while taking a deep breath. "I mean, come on, Celine. You know that this is basically the only thing I have. I'm not athletic—my best mile time is seven minutes and thirty-two seconds, while Robert's is six, and I'm not aesthetically pleasing to anyone. I'm a total klutz. Have you forgotten what happened in computer music?"

Celine burst out laughing. "That's still funny."

I rolled my eyes at her and seriously considered flipping her off before continuing. "And I'm the least respected singer in advanced choir, so grades are the only thing I can be good at," I said. I bit my lip.

"Look. It doesn't matter what you're good at as long as you're a good person. I mean, you're nice, funny, a bit too dark . . . "

"Oh, shut up."

"But still! It doesn't matter if you didn't get a 100 on the math test because there's always next time. Life isn't a numbers game. Life is about learning to give a shit where it's deserved."

"That's the cheesiest crap I've ever heard you say."

Chapter 4

Spanish flew by with its usual crap: complete three workbook pages, select an activity from said pages, and create a video containing the lines from the activity you selected. But something felt . . . off. I just felt this weird vibe emanating from Celine. That last line she said—it just didn't sit well with me. It felt as if she was subtly implying that, at particular moments, I wasn't deserving of her care. I kept trying to push the thought out of my head, telling myself I was being absolutely delusional and irrational, but it etched itself into my brain. Even though she looked over her shoulder to make deranged faces at me and smile, the thought of my best friend leaving me was everlasting—as if a Sharpie wrote the thought on my brain.

Then, the memories seeped back into my mind again like they always did when I was afraid.

It's not like I completely forgot about them, and I knew it would happen eventually. They just caught me off guard. I mean, of all times to start thinking of hanging yourself with a computer cord again, why during Spanish? They just started playing in my head one by one, and I couldn't stop myself from seeing the same scenes over and over again. I knew them inside and out, line for line, even though I haven't thought about them for a year or so. Even though I tried to repress them. Even though I tried to ignore the voices in my head that repeated the insults back to me.

Even though I tried to stop believing that their remarks about me were true.

NOVEMBER 18, 2012

Sometimes, I seriously question the choir teacher's authority. I mean, of all the guys who tried out for chamber choir, why did I get in? I mean, was he half-drunk when he was evaluating me? I honestly thought that when I sang it sounded like a dying cat on drugs, but my friends begged to differ. There could be only one reason he let me in. Conspiracy Theory #1: I was quite the teacher's pet in sixth grade, so the only reason why I got into zero period choir was because of my knowledge of music theory. It genuinely sucked to be in choir based on academic music merit because you knew you would never get solos. Another thing to get bashed about. Another difference.

"So, are you naturally a crappy singer, or did it take time for you to get where you are?"

I glanced over my shoulder to see Sevian staring at me with his most supercilious face, rolling his thin, brown eyes back. His bushy eyebrows furrowed up as if he were genuinely curious to hear my answer instead of mocking me: *If this short, entitled, blond douchebag wants to treat upperclassmen like this, he's got another thing coming.*

Wait.

Just leave.

Don't buy into it.

He wants to be a pain in the ass, let him be a pain in the ass. He'll learn.

I took a deep breath and kept walking down the hallway toward the curb.

"Oh, silence. Do you think you're too good to speak to me? I mean, you already know I'm gonna get the part? Did you really think you were going to?" Sevian said while following.

I stopped and turned around to face him. "Look, Dude," I said while putting my hands up. "I already knew I wasn't gonna get the part because I don't have the vocal range for the character, and I don't have a lisp. I cannot portray a seven-year-old because I'm a bass. Is that what you needed to hear for your ego?" I expected him to be ashamed and look down at the concrete floor when I was done admitting my beliefs, but as I finished I saw a wide smile spread across his face.

"Thanks for admitting you're not even good enough to get a side character role. I just wanted to make sure you weren't in a state of denial."

OCTOBER 18, 2013

They kept pointing at me, and I could tell they were scrutinizing me as I casually ate my stale macaroni and cheese from the cafeteria. They started to whisper amongst each other, but I could still hear them. Chris, the taller of the two, singled me out as he lifted his tanned arm and initiated conversation to John, his fellow asshole, while he peered at me from under his stringy hair that almost covered one of his eyes.

"He's gotta be gay, right?"

"Well, no duh," John replied while rolling his brown eyes and touching up the gelled, curly bush that was his hair. "He's hanging out with a crapload of girls like a true faggot."

I could feel the heat building up behind my eyes, and I started to sniffle.

"Yo, Michael." Chris said. I looked up at him, trying to look confident. "I know you can't even score two points in basketball like a true guy, but you wanna head to the bathroom and strip?" Chris and John started laughing before Chris continued. "I'm ready whenever you are."

Shit. These two bitches, thinking they have authority over everything because they come from some rich Asian descent, were getting the better of me.

I tried to resist, holding back the heat forming from behind my eyes; I knew Chris and John well enough, since we encountered each other in the same second-grade class five years ago, to know this was how they acted—menacing and poking at people's weak spots for fun and games. I tried to stare down those two pairs of oval, almond-colored eyes that mocked me for as long as I could to feign resilience against these crude, superficial comments, but I couldn't keep up the act.

I could feel the tears streaming down my cheeks one by one as I bit my lip and turned the other way. As I wiped my eyes, Celine began to reply.

"You're just jealous he can talk to girls and you can't," she snarked back.

"Why would I be jealous of not being able to bang someone without dying?" Chris shot back.

I thought the river inside me was done pouring out, but the currents were unstoppable. I buried my face as I turned back around and then put my forehead upon my forearms, which lay on the table.

"No girl would probably want to bang you, period, Douchebag. With a bigoted mouth like that, you'll probably drive every girl away."

"Whatever, Fat Bitch," Chris said as he walked to a table with John.

"You okay?" Celine asked after a momentary delay while putting her hand on my back. She knew I wasn't, but she didn't know any other way to make me feel better.

I didn't respond. If I had known that Celine would feel responsible for my anxiety later on, I would have, but you only get one chance at things in life, and maybe it's because the universe is a bastard and wants people to feel helpless and have regret as long as they breathe. I think that's why I can't trust Celine sometimes. Because I feel like she can't stand the thought of seeing someone she has negatively affected all the time. Because I don't think she can handle all the negative attention that people throw at her for being associated with me—the constant interrogation, subtle insults.

Because I know she'll eventually start believing what everyone says about me and turn against me.

I could feel Celine's eyes focus on me for a while after she asked. She was eating her homemade peanut-butter-and-jelly sandwich when I lifted my head from the table, and she kept glancing over at me to make sure I wasn't going to lose it again.

I think that was the only moment I believed she sincerely cared for me and that she wasn't comforting me because of some ulterior motive, the only time where I felt there was one person in the world who wasn't trying to fuck me over.

MAY 26, 2015

After warming up and singing songs for the pop concert, zero period choir ended, and I had to get my books for homeroom, first, and second period. Homeroom was supposed to be for silent reading, but I usually didn't read my book. I thought about how the school was society and how everyone survived in this hellhole. Through all the bullying, tormenting, and taunting, I've never changed. And that wasn't the best school survival plan. The bell screeched through the classroom, and I headed toward the locker rooms.

P. E. was the bane of my existence. It was the core reason why I've picked up the knife so many times and thought about thrusting it straight through my chest. All seventh and eighth graders met up on the boiling blacktop after they got dressed. Today we were supposed to participate in ultimate Frisbee.

"Why are we even playing? It's just us two against the entire field."

Were they blind? I'm running my ass off over here, wide open for a catch, but they overlook me. Am I really that insignificant? That invisible?

I again waved my arms with resentment to signal that I was open to catch, but Ian and Levian had tunnel vision and a lack of trust due to their close history since the idiots were two years old. The only people they could pass to, they believed, were each other. So Levian, in possession of the Frisbee after the opposing team scored another point, tossed it to Ian. After barely grasping it from the person guarding him, Ian waited for Levian to run across the field so he could pass it forward.

I looked at Levian and Ian in the distance and realized how foolish I was; I was ignorant to think they could notice someone they only knew for half a semester (the first time we met was this year on the basketball courts for P. E. roll call), but I knew that was also just how everyone treated me—like I was a total stranger and that my presence didn't warrant anything.

Negligible is the only word you could have used to describe how I was feeling. I was a miniscule fly. Wait, no—flies get more attention than I did, even with their reputation of carrying disease and sickness. I was a tiny speck of dust that couldn't even be noticed in an idiotic P. E. sport. A hell of a life I was living. I was merely taking up space and air that could be used to fill the world with TVs or trains or bridges or phones, you know? Things that actually matter. Because, apparently, I didn't.

I sighed as I put my head down and walked the opposite direction my team was supposed to be heading in order to score a goal. It's not like they would notice, right?

The bell rang after fifty-five minutes, but the fact that I was so insignificant that I was overlooked will be remembered forever. That I wasn't good enough to even be noticed. And it was even worse because I was a guy, and I was supposed to be athletic. But I was different from most. Disliked for it by my own gender. It was like treason, going against the current. And I kept drowning in the direction I was going. I didn't want to conform to society's ways. I couldn't.

Chapter 5

MAY 27, 2015

The mask. We all wear it. Those parts that people don't like, that don't fit into the crowd, we conceal behind a fake part of ourselves. Giving up part of our authenticity to be accepted into school didn't seem worth it. Not to mention the result: thinking that fabricated part of our mask is actually us.

I strolled over to biology, and after countless glances at the clock while taking notes on evolution, class ended.

I know it sounds hard to believe, but I despised snack break and lunch. It was the social essence of it all. This is where the popularity is proven, athleticism is shown, and bullying begins, especially for me, being one of only two guys who hung out predominantly with girls. It was strenuous, and the deck was stacked against me.

Sucked crap at singing, couldn't even swing a baseball bat, and essentially only hung out with girls. Oh, what a life I was having. For me, it was easier to talk to girls since: 1) They watched more TV shows that the majority of guys, and I obsessed over the shows as much as the girls did; 2) I was just as unathletic as they were except I can sprint faster; and 3) they didn't talk about only games and sports.

I could hear the whispers of hell. The words that stung like a bullet seemed to be louder:

Gay

Loser

Not gonna amount to anything

What a nobody!

The knife was already dripping with blood, but someone continuously stabbed me with each painstaking word. Each word was said numerous times by numerous people, multiplying the negativity, making me believe that I didn't deserve to exist. My footing was slipping from the world.

Chapter 6

"You ever feel like you're disappearing?" asked Meredith.

"All the time," I said in unison with Izzie.

As all the main interns at TV's Seattle Grace Hospital left for work, I finished checking my pre-algebra homework. I felt abandoned, and, at the same time, I felt like everyone was out to get me.

Vulnerability was a constant feeling for me. Bullets sliced the air to get to me, and I had no defenses. My walls were torn down by one of the only feelings I ever felt all the time: inferiority. It was unsafe to go to school, unsafe to invest in a relationship, and unsafe to trust.

"Guys, wait up!" I said.

"Run faster!" Rebekah whispered to three of my other friends as the wind picked up her frizzy, long, brown hair.

They were too quick. I had no possibility of catching up. As they sprinted to finish their lap and I saw them get smaller and smaller, I thought:

What's wrong with me? Why am I not good enough for them? Will I ever be extraordinary?

My pace slowed to a walk, and I never interacted with anyone again unless they spoke first. I couldn't handle the risk of being caught alone.

The day dragged by, each hour seeming to be slower than the last. As the show subtitles disappeared from the bottom half of my computer screen, dinner slowly approached.

You know how people who work for someone else live the same relative day over and over and over again? That was already me. I worked for my depression.

It told me everyday: *Go heat up your crappy food that your mother only made because she has to!* or: *They don't love you; they never will. Get that through your thick skull*, or, the one I heard the most: *No one gives a damn. Give hope up. It's just there to disappoint.*

Depression was my boss, so I had to listen and believe what it told me while I read books for half the day and binge-watched Netflix for the other half.

I wanted to starve to death, but my mother would notice if the food went untouched. So after drearily microwaving my food and eating it in front of my computer screen, I brushed my teeth, took a shower, and got into bed. I snatched my journal from the counter beside me and wrote.

Kill Self?

27 May 2015

To me,

Meredith Grey said that most of the lonely people come from the hospital. The endless work hours end up in barely any time for a life outside the hospital. Not only the people from the hospital are lonely, but the ones who are concerned about them are lonely as well. I've come to a conclusion that loneliness wouldn't matter. Not when there are plenty of instruments to stop that feeling. Gun is the quickest way to go. I wish I could buy one, but I don't have enough money for one and I'm not of age yet. Of course, knife is another path, but it is not always certain that loneliness will stop if I use one.

Today, I had the realization that he doesn't care about me anymore. He doesn't need me. I already addressed this problem, and he says he cares, but does he really? Anyone can lie through text message. After all, he's been purposely neglecting me and he has better people. I will always be last, even though we just met. I don't know why I'm still friends with him. I don't know why I keep relapsing into this endless cycle of: He's using you, *and:* He couldn't give two shits about you. *Maybe it's because I still have hope, but it's a tiny shred, and he keeps smashing it into smaller pieces. Maybe it's because I poured my secrets into him and I wanted him to trust me just as much. Maybe it's because he was one of the only people there for me. It's because Meredith said it herself, that even if it's the most painful thing someone could do, it's better to be with someone than be lonely. I told him how he could show he cares, but he never does it.*

"I do care about you" is just an empty remark.

He probably thought of me as an annoying, obsessive, clingy, vapid bitch. I wasn't good enough for him. He could never like me. I knew that it was too good to be true. To think that an older guy like Adam could actually be friends with me . . . everyone was out to destroy me.

After I finished the journal entry, I lay in bed for a while, thinking about how many people or activities were ahead of me in Adam's list of priorities. Once I got to number fifty-five, who was probably someone in my grade who was on his sports team, I fell asleep.

I observed him, his muscular build that he developed from basketball, his calm, welcoming eyes that I also saw Celine have sometimes—except in a shade of brown—and the way he sat with confidence. But then I noticed his negligence, ignorance, and annoyance toward me; all this negativity he built for me, even though we only knew each other for three months because we had the same elective of computer music, which maybe was for the worst.

He vented to his friends about how I always said hi everyday and how it was irritating. To me, if someone cared enough about me to talk to me every chance they got, that would mean a lot, because it would show that they have my back, and that was what I was trying to show him. But that's not what he saw.

" . . . Socially awkward . . .weird . . . obsessive . . . attached . . . bothersome . . . acting like we're dating . . . obviously gay . . . the rumors were true." That's the kind of stuff I overheard him saying to his friends.

That shattered me into a million broken pieces. To think that the one person I thought who actually genuinely cared about me tried just as much, if not even more, to outcast and bash me. Then, I saw him receive a text from me and one of my friends, Samantha. As he slid Samantha's text message toward the right and replied, my eyes filled with light. Hope. But he turned off his phone immediately afterwards and ignored my text. I knew where I stood. I knew that I didn't matter, even though I told him that he saved me once, how much he meant to me, but now he's also one of the people who broke me.

My life was a living hellish nightmare. As I woke up from my dream, I saw it was 3:00 a.m. I sat up and slowly brought my legs to my chest. After wrapping my arms around them and interlacing my fingers, I buried my face into my knees. Warm tears started to drip onto the bed sheet. They constantly rolled down, faster and faster, and I hyperventilated with each drop.

Life sucks.

There's no hope.

Nothing turns out great.

Wake up from this nightmare by never waking up.

Chapter 7

It was all I could think about.

It takes one stab, one gulp, one rope, or one jump to kill myself. My mind taunted me with relentless comments about it.

The blood will make you feel better. The water you're sinking under will ease the pain. The lack of breath will make you feel alive. Your choking will wake you up.

I fantasized about it: My hand slowly coming out of the ocean and ultimately sinking back under the currents. My entire body, flailing under waves of suffocation and then, ultimately, gradually, stopping with no movement whatsoever. Blood dripping from my chest as I lay on the floor. A cup rolling away from my hand and sprawled body with toxic fluid spilled across the carpet.

I couldn't fall back asleep. Twisting and turning, I tried to find the last position I slept in, but even when I found a comfortable one, my eyes refused to stay closed. I couldn't stop thinking about jumping off the San Francisco bridge or drinking detergent or tying a rope around my neck or stabbing myself. It seemed delectably irresistible.

I threw aside my blanket and jumped out of bed. After walking over the carpet and pulling open the wooden door, I alertly snuck over the chilly tile floor toward the kitchen. I opened the drawer quietly and looked at the objects with hope. I shuffled through the knives until I found the perfect one. It had an extremely sharp blade that was about four and a half inches with approximately fifteen thorny teeth. I took out the knife sharpener and dragged my knife in one direction across it. I held the black metal handle in my hand, studying the shiny surface. I trudged back to my room, tossing the knife from hand to hand, as if I had done this before since I thought about it frequently. I grinned at the thoughts that were surfacing to my mind. This would be the pill I had to take only once to end all pain. As I got back in bed and placed the knife under my pillow, I drifted to sleep in a few seconds as the presence of the knife gave me reassurance.

THURSDAY, MAY 28, 2015

I woke up to find that my mom's silver Honda minivan wasn't parked in our backyard. She didn't give a crap about me. That's why she didn't come home. It's because she hated me. Everything I did was wrong. Every breath was sinful. After washing my face, brushing, changing clothes, and shoving my backpack with homework, I slid the knife into my pocket. The handle protruded slightly, so I changed shirts and wore a larger one to cover it. Then, I seized my journal from the wooden counter and placed it in my backpack. I got my house key, chained to a Dalek lanyard, and walked outside with my backpack. While locking the door and putting on my Converse,

I remembered that I would have to take my shorts off for P. E. so I could change. I took the knife out and instead, put it into a small pocket in my backpack. I slung the backpack over my shoulder again and started walking.

Have you ever felt lonely even though you were in a room filled with people? That was me, all the time. That feeling is even worse when you're walking alone on a sidewalk at 6:15 in the morning with cars vrooming by. The thing about walking solo on a street bursting with cars early in the morning is that there are so many people, but they don't notice you. People don't even glance at you. They rush by as if you're nothing. You're miniscule. Overlooked. Unimportant. Unwanted. Unnecessary. Nonexistent. In a cramped room, at least some people might take a peek at you. Maybe say hi. Possibly talk about you in a good or bad way, but at least you're noticed. On the streets, you're basically a ghost.

At 6:30, I reached the middle school to see desolate halls. I ambled to my locker and threw my backpack in. After taking my folder out and slamming my locker shut, I kicked my locker three times out of frustration and sat against it. Sweltering tears started to make my folder a darker shade of grey, but I tried to make no sound. I could feel my face heat up and redden. I'm a failure. A nobody. Today was tryout day for pop concert solos and I knew, for sure, that I would not get any of them. I wiped the now warm tears from my face and folder with my sleeve. I hugged my knees, rested my head on top of my choir folder, and stared stone-faced at the bustling cars flashing past the school. I desired that—to flash by and be gone in an instant. I also wanted to be remembered as more than just a passing moment, but I knew I could never achieve that.

The choir teacher finally arrived and unlocked the door to the choir room. I stood up and trudged toward the room while Mr. Helinski walked in with his glasses resting on his nose to protect his brown eyes instead of his usual colored contacts. As I followed him in, I persuaded myself not to try out for any of the solos so I wouldn't have to suffer the inevitable outcome: disappointment. Silently, I took my place on the risers and waited for the rest of the class to stream in. Mr. Helinski started the auditions at 7:00 a.m. Person after person stood up to sing and recite lines in front of the class, as the pop concert was in a play form. During each student's tryout, Mr. Helinski scratched his head, and with it his receding hairline, to signify profound thought while he kept crinkling and looking over his thin pale nose.

"Michael, would you like to try out?" Mr. Helinski asked me.

I shook my head in response.

I could hear Billy whisper to his friend, "Probably because he finally realized he sucks crap at singing," and they both obnoxiously laughed.

I just looked down at my shoes for the remainder of class and silently choked back sobs.

After zero period ended, Josh came up to me and whispered in my ear, "Hey, Michael. Why don't we both go into the bathroom and do things that we shouldn't be doing?" He chuckled as he walked away.

I wanted to be Carrie at the prom, to take my vengeance and obtain redemption on this sick school and kill the lowlife bastards who had been stabbing me with the blades of their words. Simultaneously, though, I felt like I was a humongous building during an earthquake with a magnitude of 8.9, crumbling and falling apart. Both Carrie and I had one quality in common already: we were both blood-soaked. Except in the movie of my life, I was the one being murdered, while Carrie was the murderess in hers.

I wanted the day to rush by and leave me behind. I didn't want to remember this pain later in the day. I didn't want to give people more opportunities to damage me. I wanted to be left alone so no one could harm me. But instead, I was getting dragged to my death slowly by time.

After almost punching my locker in front of people, and being on the edge of having an emotional breakdown, I picked up my books and binders and sauntered toward homeroom. Instead of thinking for twenty minutes about how cliques influence people's behavior by requiring them to alter, I propped my book up in the teacher's direction so she couldn't see me. I snagged my journal from my stack of books and took out one of my pencils.

Kill Self?

28 May 2015

To me,

I have seen pain lurking in every corner I turn. He couldn't care less about me, there is no one to depend on, and I'm slowly being degraded till I don't exist. It's not like me to write an entry during the day, but maybe this is the feeling that Meredith Grey had. I just felt like I was going to die today. Hopefully, I'm not going to find some homemade bomb in a patient I'm treating that is bound to explode at any second, but sometimes, I wish I was. If the world is all about crushing confidence and burning trust, then the school is doing a helluva good job preparing us for it.

Homeroom ended in chatter louder than the bell's screech. On my way down the cement stairway toward the lunch court, I caught Adam's glance. We both held each other's eyes while walking till we passed each other, but neither of us said anything. Great. I was not even worth the breath of saying hi. Then, I glanced back to see Samantha cheerfully greeting him with a response in return. As I advanced to the metallic blue tables, my eyes started to water, but I rubbed my eyes to try to wipe the disappointment away.

The problem with being suicidally depressed is that it's extremely hard to keep up the facade of being completely normal. So although I didn't necessarily alter my personality in order to be accepted into society, I still had to be fake, but on top of that, I still got picked on. It basically sucks either way: either you believe in fake authenticity in order to not be ostracized by society, and ultimately believe that is your true self while you try to please everyone but yourself; or, stay true to yourself but still be cast out because of it, which can ultimately lead to your downfall. Pick your poison.

Chapter 8

I slowly rolled a pencil out of my bag and took a seat on top of the painted number assigned to me on the searing blacktop. As the rest of the class squatted above their numbers, the P. E. teachers passed out small wooden clipboards to write on top of and a Scantron—a vertically positioned answer sheet for a multiple-choice test, covered with lettered bubbles to fill in with number-two pencil. After Mr. Bernard shouted what to write on the subject line and the date while putting on a sunhat to cover his grey hairs, he passed out the three-part test and looked us individually through his plain black sunglasses. It was hilariously ironic. I may suck crap in the field of athletic ability, but I knew more of the material than top jocks. I was the first to finish in seventh grade, and the second one to finish overall right behind Adam.

Once I gave Mr. Bernard the Scantron, Ms. Tang the wooden slide, and Coach John all three parts to the test, I had to walk the circular dirt track. Adam glanced behind and saw me, but he didn't even acknowledge my presence. He didn't stop to let me catch up to him, and I knew that if I jogged to get to him, he wouldn't actually enjoy talking to me. So we both walked by ourselves, until one of Adam's friends ran to him and they started chattering.

I walked alone, balancing myself on top of the small sliver of concrete near the oval grass field in the middle of the track. I thought to myself: *This is basically how all suicidal people walk through life. We slip constantly, trying to regain balance in life but it never lasts for long. We do this until we break, snap, and lean one way or the other. And it's so easy to go either way or get back on the border between the two.*

Once the bell rang and everyone was finished with their finals, I snatched my stuff from the lunch tables and waited beneath the arch. I stared blankly at the bright blue sky with fluffy clouds for a while and then walked to biology.

Mrs. Keaning was too lazy to put together a final, so she announced to the class that the grades we currently had were the ones we were stuck with, all the while staring at pictures of her two cats on her iPhone. She also told the class that although we were taking chapter twelve notes, we weren't going to have a chapter twelve test. So instead of doing multiple guess for the second period in a row, Mrs. Keaning put on G-rated Disney movie, as the school required teachers not show any movies with a higher rating, and I grabbed my journal and a pencil.

How many missed opportunities has he gotten? I've passed him countless times in the hall, but it's as if I was as unimportant as the copyright pages in a book right beside the title page—they only matter until you need them. I want to talk to him, but every time I do, he never cares enough to carry the conversation along or neglects me altogether. No wonder I keep falling back into relapse with him. He never follows through with what he says he'll do; his actions never support his thoughts. I still keep thinking he's going to change to make me happy, but I now realize that I wasn't even worth changing for.

After I sandwiched my journal between my binder and pencil bag, I seized the opportunity to watch my first Disney movie. People told me it was tragic that I've never seen a Disney movie. They said it would scar my childhood, not being able to see the glee and whimsy of one, but I begged to differ. I'd much rather have watched a movie I could relate to, one that was dark and twisty.

Snack break began in an instant after the drone of the bell. As I escaped class through the green door, oceans of people passed by. After getting my materials out for third and fourth period, I shut my locker and walked to the lunch court. Once I was amid the rows of metallic blue tables, I couldn't find my friends. After scouting around for about two whole minutes, I spotted them in a corner far from where we usually sit. When I sat down, they all got up and sprinted away from me. I chased after them, knowing for a fact that I run faster than all of them. I grabbed the hood of my friend Chloe and pulled her to me.

"What the hell is wrong? Why are you guys trying to avoid me?" I asked her.

"We can't have someone who's gay in our group," she replied while she glared at me with her brown eyes through her straightened-out black hair.

I let go of her hood in awe. It might have been anger or despair, but I just let go. I stood there, frozen, staring at my so-called friends who were getting smaller and smaller as they walked away, until they turned and sat down at a table next to the arch. What a familiar feeling. I gulped back the lump in my throat, and walked back to where my books were and sat down. I wasn't hungry, and I realized I was just an object everyone could make fun of.

I should've realized it was coming. My friends would talk amongst each other, excluding me. Like they were planning that moment for days, weeks, or even months. And the feeling was so familiar, because I remember it so vividly the first time, but it hurt even more this time because I was friends with these backstabbers for longer and I trusted them more. Maybe you can't really trust anyone, though.

People dissed me whenever they could. In social studies, the teacher told the people in the front row to get textbooks for their row, and I had to get one myself. In Spanish, my red pen ran out of ink and I asked my neighbor if I could borrow one, but she just ignored me. And at the end of the day, I came back to a locker full of sticky-notes with hell written all over them.

People in my school said seventh grade sucked crap. I can confidently support that. The taunting, the tormenting, the insecurity, the exponentially heavier workload compared to sixth grade: it was a hard transition. And it was so hard to survive. Sometimes, we didn't.

I came home with an urge to write in my journal. After shuffling through my black and dark blue backpack, I took out the red velvet book that held all my insecurities in it. I took a seat on a wooden stool in front of my computer.

All alone without a shoulder to lean on. I should've stopped letting people feed my friends and everyone who knows me a rumor that was false. Now, they've heard it enough times to believe it. And now, if people who've known me for six years don't really know who I am and have abandoned me, is there really anyone who has faith in me?

I stopped gripping the pencil and opened my hand. I walked over to a counter where I had a first place trophy for a tennis competition. I clenched my hand around it and held it up against the light. There it was. Achievement. I hugged it against my chest—it was the only thing that could give me comfort. My eyes started to water. I needed an object to give me validation.

I threw the golden trophy toward the wall and the glass figurine of a man doing an overhand serve shattered into hundreds of pieces, and the plastic columns he had stood on fell to the floor. I dropped to my knees and sobbed into my hands.

Chapter 9

FRIDAY, MAY 29, 2015

It's hard to put on a facade of happiness and glee when you know no one will buy it anymore; when you know that people assume you've broken down thousands of times and you're losing it, yet they keep talking about you; when all that goes on in your head is the exact opposite of how you try to act; when you only think of what people say about you, and then those thoughts become permanent.

School wasn't really school anymore for me. It was more like hell. Demons cornered me every minute I was there. Thousands of opportunities opened for them to keep killing me, and killing me, and killing me. I was already so bruised, but they keep on beating my dead corpse. The only way to stop my endless suffering was to actually die.

Kill Self?

29 May 2015

To me,

What the damn hell was I thinking two days ago when I thought that everything was falling apart? It had already fallen apart. All of it. The building already collapsed. It's just debris now. I'm not even a person any more. I'm just something to play around in after breaking and to discard after enough fun has been had.

But what if they're never satisfied? What if they just want to play with me like a toy that they never get tired of? I don't want to give hope anymore chances to let me down. I don't want to hope that people get tired of me and just forget about me. I want to know that they'll get tired of me and forget about me. Just ignore me so I can actually recover from my wounds. But that's not for certain. Why can't there always be 100 percent for sure chances? Why do people always fucking say "The struggle makes the victory that much sweeter?" What if there's never victory? What if you were always set up for failure? What if someone were me? They would've probably given up already, so what the hell am I waiting for? Nothing, because there's nothing worth waiting for anymore. I've lost basically everything, and there's no one who cares about me.

After I finished writing in my journal, I walked to the kitchen to, once again, see the absence of my mom's car.

Undeserving of anything, even to my mom. Even to my friends now. Worthless is what I am.

I washed my face, brushed my teeth, placed the knife into my backpack's outside pocket again, and changed into my "Doctor Who" weeping angel shirt with grey shorts on. Walking to school for the second day in a row, I placed my journal into the second pocket of my backpack and slung it across my shoulder.

The outside greeted me with stinging cold air, and I started to trudge to school after locking the door.

Once I got to school, I froze. I pulled my phone from my pocket and checked the time. 6:30 a.m. I just stood there on the sidewalk that led to the circular curb near the office while chilly breezes swept past me. I couldn't even bear to look at the damn place. The place where I collapsed. The place where I see the people who destroyed me every day. The place that let me down countless times. The place that was always against me. The place where I can never come out on top. The place where I'm always being stepped on, where I'm always at the bottom.

I couldn't handle it. I threw my backpack to the sidewalk and sprinted behind a tree two yards away from where I stood. I leaned on the tree, acting as if it was the only thing that would always be there for me. I wrapped my arms around the trunk and started to feel something build up in my throat. I slowly started to drop to the dirt against the hard exterior of the tree. I could hear my heart pounding louder than a roller coaster. I started to take short, punctuated breaths. I couldn't take it anymore. The fact that there was nothing left was too much for me to handle. Up until then, I thought I was fine with that, but as I looked at the place that crushed me, I realized that it would be worse. It could only get worse. Nothing could turn out better.

Part Two

Standstill

Chapter 10

Last day.

That's what I kept thinking to myself as I walked to my locker. Last day, and no one needs to know. Fuck, no one would even care if it were my last day here. I snagged my choir folder from my backpack and threw my backpack into my locker after opening it. Once I slammed the locker door, I just sat alone on the cement hallway floor. I stared out the window at the sky and thought to myself: *I'll be there soon.*

It was hard to keep thinking *I'll leave* when everything started to unfold. And for some reason, when it unfolded, it miraculously started to turn out extraordinarily. It had been forever since I'd thought that of something: extraordinary, especially about a day. When I approached the choir room door, I saw my name, for some reason, right next to a solo. Once Mr. Helinski finally got to school, I asked him why my name was next to the solo when I never tried out for anything. He explained that he thought I was more fit for the solo than the guys who tried out if he remembers my voice correctly from the last time he heard me sing. I didn't get in because of pity. I didn't get in because he needed a student to help others with music theory sheets. I actually had something to contribute to the choir voice-wise, which enabled me to stop the facade and actually be it. For the first time in a while, I could be genuinely perky.

All the teachers were required to hand back their last finals to the students today. I scored a 95% for world history, 100% for P. E., 97% for English, 92% for math, and 98% for Spanish. I ended up raising all of my grades exponentially. Excellence by obtaining solos, by thriving in academic terms (which I've had before in the last three quarters but obtaining it even while being focused on demeaning verbal harassment made me feel even more proud). It was kinda great.

Instead of being trapped in purgatory, it felt like I was actually above ground and there was no possible way I could be buried under again. It felt exhilarating, and for the first time in awhile, I wanted to live.

After school, I walked home and looked back to see that Adam was right behind me with his friends and girlfriend. He noticed me and waved. That was one seized opportunity out of thousands, but that would suffice for me. I turned all the way around and waved back with a smile. He smiled back, but then kept talking to Denise, his girlfriend. I turned back around and kept walking. I couldn't help smiling the rest of the way home. I wasn't a one-night stand to make Adam feel better about himself. He still cared about me, and that felt fucking great.

As I walked in the driveway next to my house, I saw my mom's car parked in the backyard. I rushed up the cement stairs and quickly unlocked and slid the glass door to the right so I could walk in. I took off my shoes and came to see my mom talking on the phone in the family room. It felt so vast now that someone else was in the room beside just me alone. She had a gigantic grin across her face after hanging up. She put her hand in her pocket and produced two tickets for a Halsey concert at the Forum, section 124, row 1, seats 1–2. The seats were basically touching the side of the stage, and all I could do to thank my mom was smile. Once it was 6:00 p.m., I got into my mom's car, riding shotgun as she pulled out of the driveway.

"Are you glad that I was home?" my mom asked.

"Yeah! But why did you come?" I asked.

"I already filled in eighty hours this week, which is the new maximum for surgeons at the hospital. So I had to take mandatory time off."

So much for a great day. My mom couldn't even drive herself away from her job to see me unless it was state law. That sucked crap, and the rest of the drive was deafening with silence. As I slammed the car door and walked around the gigantic circular building that was the Forum with my mom, I couldn't help thinking that I liked it better when she didn't come home at all, so I didn't have to know that she was forced to spend time with her only son.

School might be almost over, and I skeptically believed that being talked about by the entire school might stop soon and would stop permanently, but it felt like everything was just going to freeze for just a moment, and then it would melt and fall again. I just wanted this day, this rare phenomenal day, to last an entire year. But I kept thinking as Halsey sang her new album, "Badlands," that it would be a steep, downward drop to the ground once school started. I kept hoping that wouldn't happen, that dirt wouldn't just pile on top of me and make me a dead boy walking.

The next two days passed by like leaves falling in autumn—slowly and sadly. It was kinda hard to believe the school year was coming to an end. I mean, I wanted it to end—to have a period of rest from the teasing—but I didn't want to end the school year alone. That meant I'd be like the new kid next year, but no one would want to welcome me and I wouldn't be mysterious and cool, like how most new students are.

MONDAY, JUNE 1, 2015

School didn't feel like school anymore. There was no education whatsoever. It dwindled down to fun and games. We watched *Finding Nemo* in social studies, played Four Corners in English, and had free time in P. E. But most of all, school didn't feel like school because the pointing stopped. The whispers stopped. And it felt like time stopped. Because, I guess, school was ending and everyone was either excited or sad because they'd miss their friends. They had no time for me. And for the first time, it felt great that everyone in school didn't have time for me.

I'd rather be left alone by the people I love than spend time with the people I hate. It was basically the exact opposite of what Meredith Grey said, that you should stay with people even if it was the hardest thing to do.

After sixth period ended, the first rehearsal for the pop concert started. It felt nerve-racking—the thought of people hearing my voice alone for the first time. I felt my voice would crack on the high notes, and that I wouldn't be able to hit the low notes. After Mr. Helinski reviewed the order of songs, we practiced walking on and off the risers for the songs that involved all choirs. Then, the advanced choir would performance two songs and next would be my solo. *It's going to be all right*, I told myself. There's nothing to be afraid of. Except I knew I was lying to myself. Everything was frightening. My voice could dramatically change and sound gruesomely bad. Not only would I be the talk of the school after that, but that would carry on until next year. "Seasons of Love" and "For Good", the two songs the advanced choir sang, seemed to fly by.

Before I knew it, it was just me on the stage. As I stepped off the risers to approach the mic, it seemed to taunt me. Little words of insecurity started to appear on the stand and the mic itself. I tried to ignore the words and opened my mouth as the music started, but I found myself afraid of making a sound.

It's just your insecurity. Just insecurity. People will love your voice and people will talk about how great it is. Don't be afraid. There's nothing to be scared of.

I thought the solo went great, but people became utterly silent afterward. I didn't know if it was because I was so bad it was shocking, or if it was because I did so well they were surprised. But it didn't matter; I would find out what people thought of me on Thursday.

Once the 5:30 bell rang, Mr. Helinski grabbed me from the ocean of people leaving the auditorium to tell me I did great. He probably told me that to comfort me, to make sure I didn't back out of the solo by worrying myself to death about what people think. It was just like he always said during zero period. Sing out, because you have nothing to prove to anyone here. Just an empty reassurance.

The cracked sidewalk greeted me with open arms. I'd walked it for so long by now I thought: *it's going to miss me when I graduate*. But graduation would take one more year. One more year for a fresh start away from this hellish prison.

I came home to an empty house. There wasn't really anything to do. With no finals left to study for, I had an exceedingly awkward amount of free time. School was basically all I had. It was everything I was good at. I wasn't excellent at piano and tennis; I was just better than the average person. I was still mediocre compared to basically half the people in my school who did those activities. But with academics stopping for three months, I realized the only thing I would do would be watching Netflix or reading books. So the cost for people to stop talking about me was that I wouldn't be able to do the one thing I was superior at, the one thing that gave me indomitable confidence.

THURSDAY, JUNE 4, 2015

It was terrifying, even just standing on the risers in a group—the lights, the heat, and the eyes. The lights shone on me unwaveringly, sweat trickled down my head and reminded me of how nervous I was at every second, and silhouetted heads stared back at me. It was all just frightening. *Am I blending well? Oh crap, did I hold that note out too long? Freaking hell, did I sing too loud when we were supposed to be piano?* I just kept forgetting everything, seeming out of place. I didn't remember if I was smiling, and I was supposed to look like I was having the time of my life.

I didn't want the first song after intermission to start. If I couldn't stand with a group of about 150 people, how would I be able to sing without breaking down? But before I knew it, fifteen minutes went down the drain and all three choirs lined up to sing the opening song. Then, the beginning and intermediate choirs left the auditorium and then it was just the advanced choir. And then it was only me. Alone, isolated, and, soon to be, buried.

Their eyes didn't seem to flicker away from me as the rest of the choir got off row by row. Mr. Helinski gestured me to come down, and I stepped off the risers onto the stage as if it were a minefield.

Inhale. Exhale.

Those were the only two words that came to mind as the music started. The only two things I could do in that moment. I felt petrified. But as my opening came closer and closer, it felt easier than I thought. This was my own piece. I was my own conductor. I could do anything I wanted. Well, as long as I didn't use the cuss words in the song.

Afterward, people waved good-bye even though they barely talked to me, saying I did a great job, sometimes even extraordinary. But it didn't feel great when no one you cared about came, or when no one you cared about said congratulations. And when Adam came out of the auditorium with his girlfriend on his arm and didn't speak a word, didn't even indicate he saw me, it felt even worse. It was a great solo, but no one saw it.

As people started to leave, I just stared at my phone, waiting to get a text from my mom, saying that she at least could be able to pick me up. But when one minute turned to five, and then fifteen, I realized that I should've started walking home the moment the concert was finished.

Walking home during the day after school or before school to get to zero period on time was fine. There were plenty of cars in the streets during the morning and lots of people walking over to Starbucks or some crap during the afternoon. But walking home during the night—I had never done that before. It was so frightening. I was more prone to danger, rapists, anything and everything. But all I did was walk and listen to Halsey. I just looked at the empty dark shops and sang along with her newest album, "Badlands." I wasn't scared, and I didn't know why. Maybe it's because I thought while I was walking that I've gone through worse, and the music I was listening to was a reminder of that. A normal person would have turned on the flash on their iPhone, or kept their phone on constantly to use their screen brightness to see where they were going. But I just played music while my phone was in my pocket, embracing the darkness around me, as if it were my friend. I would've been scared to death if I was thinking about the possibility that around a dreary corner, a shooter could have been waiting to kill me.

FRIDAY, JUNE 5, 2015

Last day of school.

I would've been all "Hell yeah!" if I wasn't so concerned about how much I would stand out even with all the clamorous people in my grade on this day, that even with everyone signing each other's yearbooks, I would still be that person alone just skimming through the year's past events. When the teachers gave out awards that I never got, I would just sit in the back, while people whispered amongst themselves about their plans for the summer and how excited they were for it. And I would've been more gleeful if I also wasn't worried about whether that was going to be me the entire year in eighth grade.

When the day was over, I knew why people talked about how school was the thing you hated until you couldn't do it anymore. I always knew but on this day, the feeling was profound. As soon as the bell rang and people rushed out, I gloomily walked over to the library and sat there, even though I wasn't waiting for a ride. School was a hellhole when I was in there, but when I looked at it from far away, I realized the hellhole took a lot of free time off my hands. I was grateful because it gave me less time to sit around and do nothing or mope. The hellhole gave me friends, but for me, the hellhole also made me lose my friends. So I alternately paced and sat around for thirty minutes while people who desired to leave the school quickly rushed eagerly by.

Just when I decided to head home, I saw Adam walking over alone. As he got closer and closer to me, words just flew out of my mouth.

"Can I talk to you?" I suddenly asked.

"Sure," Adam responded. I knew I couldn't leave it there. I knew that as awkward as I felt right now, it would be even weirder just to say never mind. Either way, I had a question I was longing to ask. He walked off the sidewalk near the library and came over by the tree where I was standing. He looked at me directly, something he's never done before.

"So, like, I know grad is supposed to be a really happy time for you, but for me it's sad because you're leaving, which I said before. But will you remember me?"

The moment I asked that I thought: *Oh crap. Now I get why the guys call me "gay"*. Because I wasn't just hanging out with the girls and being sassy; I was also emotional, and now I was sure he would get that same image of me. Even more flustered and nervous than before I asked him that question, I desperately hoped he wouldn't think of me like that even though it came off in that way.

"Yeah, I guess. I'm planning to visit, so yeah. I'll remember you."

A big smile spread across my face.

"Thanks. That's all I wanted to ask you."

He smiled back and left toward the basketball courts. Once I got home, I couldn't wipe the smile off my face. I couldn't help but think that now I was as important to him as he was to me. At least I would end the school year on one high note.

For about three months, I wouldn't see the grey cement I had walked down so many times. For about three months, I wouldn't have to hear the relentless buffoons in my class while actually attempting to learn. And for about three months, I would be at home, alone. Those three things were all I could think about as I walked past the now-crowded shops of my city. I mean, I could walk to the library during the summer, so I at least had a book to comfort me, but I was too frightened by the slim chance I would see someone from school there. If I even took one step out of my house, I exposed myself more than I needed to and I didn't want to do that. I'd already been made fun of for the parts of me I showed at school, and I didn't want to keep adding to that list. So I realized, as I saw my ex-best friends coming from Starbucks, that loneliness is a cycle. And you can easily escape it, but it's much easier to stay down there.

Summer had a sluggish pace; I could feel every minute, every second pass before me. There was absolutely nothing to do. Once I caught up on *Grey's Anatomy*, I finished two other TV shows, *Scandal* and *How to Get Away with Murder*. They were five seasons in total, but seeing how I had all the time in the world, I finished them in about one and a half weeks.

My mother stopped coming back home during the summer. It was more like she stopped coming back when I was awake. Sometimes, I could hear footsteps in the hallway and after I thought the noise was a good distance away, I would open my bedroom door and see my mother's silhouette. It felt even lonelier once I found out she couldn't even take time out during the day to visit me. She couldn't even bother to keep writing notes for me on the kitchen table. Everything that was great seemed to be more like a fluke instead of being everlasting.

I couldn't stop thinking about what was going to happen in one month. I couldn't stop thinking about whether he'd actually remember me. I couldn't stop thinking about the possibility of my friends taking me back. I couldn't stop thinking about what would happen on that first day, if anything would change, if everything would change.

SATURDAY, AUGUST 15, 2015

Riinnnggg!

Rinnngggg!

I walked to the phone after taking off my headphones and pausing the episode of *How To Get Away With Murder.*

"Hello?"

"Hi, Sweetie, it's me."

I barely recognized the voice over the phone. It'd been so long since I've heard it.

"Um, who's calling?"

"It's your mom."

Oh fuck. It's another trap. Another way for me to relapse. Another opportunity for her to get me to think she cares about me when she'll leave me like a pile of shit afterward.

"Why are you calling?"

"Because we're going to Nevada!"

"Why?"

"We're going to a seminar. It'll be fun!"

It'll be fun, she says. *Over my fucking dead body.*

"Mom, I really don't want to go. I absolutely positively do not want to be in the scorching heat of the desert while learning educational crap I can't even apply until after high school."

"You are going." I could hear my mom breathe heavily because I wasn't doing what she wanted like a good kid. "It's already paid for, so you're going even if I have to knock you unconscious and drag you across the freeway without a damn car."

"You know what? Fine. I'll freaking go, but don't blame me when you have a murderous son when you get older because he was forced to do a bunch of bullcrap while growing up."

"Pack seven sets of outside clothes, four sets of sleeping clothes, seven pairs of socks, and all that crap. I'm sick of your crappy attitude."

"Then why the hell are you taking me?"

"Because it'll be a good experience."

My mom hung up right after, and I felt so relieved that I didn't have to hear her vapid voice anymore.

Chapter 11

We drove for hours on end that passed with my phone blasting music through the aux cord of the car and the barren, desolate scenery of shriveled, lackluster mountainous terrain zooming past us. My mom ramped up the speed to seventy miles per hour. It was boring. But it was . . . relaxing, I guess.

It was an escape, like time was frozen in this film that seemed to play the same scene over and over again. There was just this cinematic feeling about long drives and loud music, to me at least. And in the movies, anything is possible—explosions, survival after cars drive off cliffs, talking insects—you name it, so I guess that's why I thought I could be happy. Just for a moment. Temporarily, I felt, as Haim jammed out with me to impossible thoughts of joy, that I was loved by my mother. I mean, she spent the money and effort to enable me to go to this seminar in Nevada, and even though I thought it was a godforsaken place of arid, scorching heat, it was a difficult task to undergo in order to get there, burning countless gallons of gas and suffering way too many hours of traffic.

Not only that, but as I spent time hiding from my insecurities and anxiety, I listened just a little bit more carefully to my music as it shuffled, and I realized that sadness was not solely inflicted upon me, that other people had issues, had trouble feeling valued and appreciated, had family problems. But as my mother pulled up to the hotel and dragged our luggage out from the trunk, I realized something else: although people might undergo the same events, they all react in their own unique way. So no one could perfectly understand me or sympathize in a way that would resonate with me, heal me. Only I could do that, and I wouldn't because I knew I didn't deserve any of that, to save myself from this hole I was falling into, no matter how many hands reached down to save me, even though there were none.

Chapter 12

"And so, the teen classes will start tomorrow and they'll have snack, lunch, and dinner breaks at the same time as the adults so the teens can interact with the adults for help with their pitch to achieve what they want. Thank you, and have a great day!" Allie, the person in charge of the teen class, ended her presentation with an overly-ecstatic smile showing all of her pearly white teeth and a subtle flip of her straightened black hair as she playfully curtsied.

Thank god that's over, I thought right after Allie exited the room. She had just finished wrapping up her explanation that the seminar I had been dragged to would be a cheesy, interactive, seven-day course where the teens would pitch to older business people about their goals in life to see whether or not the adults could help give them connections or other forms of aid. My mom and I started to walk out of the room.

"So are you excited?" my mom asked.

"Sure. Whatever."

"Don't 'whatever' me. I paid good money for this. Are you or are you not excited for the class?"

"Yeah, I'm excited, I guess."

"Okay, good. Now, take the room key and head back up to the room. I'm going to stay down here for a while and talk to some people I know."

"Fine." I headed off to the eighth floor while some of the teens were going down to the pool. My mom noticed them as well while she was walking down the stairs to talk to a colleague. I was just about to get into the elevator when she shouted my name.

"Wait, Michael!" She started to gesture toward the kids going down to the pool. I rolled my eyes in response and followed right behind them after introducing myself and asking if I could come with them.

I didn't bring my swimming shorts with me, so by the time I got to the pool with the other teens, the only thing I could do was sit on a lounge chair and watch them dive in and splash water at each other. I played on my phone for a bit, but I put it down on the glass table right next to my chair and just stared into the sky. After a while, I felt tired and my eyes slowly started to shut.

I woke up because I was suddenly moving. I turned my head around to see that I was being carried toward the pool by several of the teens in the class. I started to struggle. I tried to punch them and kick them so they knew I didn't want to do this. Then, all of a sudden, I shouted at them.

"Get the hell off of me! Fuck off, idiots! I don't want to do this!" I shouted.

They carefully set me down and I took a deep breath in. I snagged the room key and my phone and headed up to the room, but I saw my mom. She started to come toward me, furious.

"What the hell is wrong with you? You don't wanna be with the teens? Fine, then you can be with the adults. I need to drop off someone I know at the airport soon, so you're coming with me. Is that what you want?"

I stood silently.

"Get your ass back to the room so you don't make another scene."

I started to go up the stairs that led up to the lobby with my mom following behind me. She pushed the "up" button and we waited for the elevator. I looked at her and her anger didn't dissipate whatsoever. Once we got in the elevator, she smashed the "eight" button and looked at the elevator doors slowly coming to a close in front of us. She stomped toward the room once she got out and I tagged behind her. After the door opened, she shoved me in the room first and started to scream at me before slamming the door shut.

"Why the hell did you do that? Why the hell do you have to ruin everything?" my mom asked.

"If I ruin everything, then why the hell did you bring me? I didn't even want to go!"

"This was supposed to be a good experience! But you just manage to mess it up!"

"Me? I ruin everything? Do you even know my birthday? Huh?"

"Of course, I do. It's February 26th."

"Whose birthday is that? You don't even know mine! That's probably some patient's! You should know my birthday is June 17th."

"That's not true! I care about you."

"Mom, you don't even know what the hell is happening in my life."

"Fine, then. What's happening in your life?"

"I think about killing myself *everyday*," I said bluntly.

"Oh, please, Drama Queen. You're just saying that. It is very rude of you to make fun—"

"You think I'm kidding? You think that the endless tormenting at school, the fact that you barely even pay attention to me because you can't bother to find out what happens at school, let alone talk to your son once in awhile, hasn't affected me?" I pulled a knife out from my backpack. "I was planning to use this when you were in class. Kill myself during lunch, or some crap. You still think I'm lying?"

"When did that start happening?"

"So now I have your attention, don't I?"

"Why are you carrying a knife around with you? Who's hurting you at school?"

"Look in the damn mirror once in awhile, Mom. You're hurting me as well. You gave birth to me, and yet you can't even remember the day I was born."

"Just give me the names of the kids who've been hurting you and this won't ever happen again. I can talk to the principal or—"

"I don't want your help!" I screamed. "I don't want to be teased for being known as the guy who needs his mom to stand up for him!"

"This needs to stop though. Just tell me their names, and the principal can separate them from you."

"You know what? Fine. Just leave me alone and forget this ever happened. I don't want you to bring this up ever again."

"Just give me their names."

"Their names are Chris and John."

"What happened with them?

"Mom, I really don't want to relive those moments."

"If you tell me what happened, I can tell the principal what happened, and he can prevent it from occurring again."

"Fine."

After skimming over what happened with Chris, I explained to my mom what happened with John. He was the person who had planted the suicide seed in my brain. One day during lunch, John was chatting with his friends about the possibility of me being gay. Of course, he agreed there was a strong possibility I liked guys in a certain way and literally shouted out his opinion. Can you say "fucking worst day of your life"?

"Okay, I'm going to call the school right now and tell them what has happened. Go downstairs and apologize to the other teens."

"Please don't, Mom. I don't want to be known as the guy who needs his mom to stand up for him."

"You won't have that reputation. Don't worry. No one will know. Now, go downstairs and apologize."

I did what my mom said and hoped like hell nothing would be said about me being a huge tattletale in the imminent school year while walking back to the elevator.

Chapter 13

The next day, I felt like the world was pushing down on me harder than before, like tension was building and something would burst, and whether that something was good or bad, I couldn't tell. And that scared the shit outta me. I didn't know what to expect as a result of my mom telling the supervisors at school of my depression.

Anxiously, I walked to breakfast with an unbearable amount of stress and tried to calm down as I sat at an empty table in the back of the bright, lively dining hall. Most of the other teens were sitting with the adults near the front of the dining hall, laughing, smiling, and talking about what they wanted to take away from the seminar. I could hear two of them talking about how they were looking for someone with a recording studio so that they could produce music, while my unambitious self sat alone and played around with my food.

One of the teens—a slender, tall guy with stringy black hair and dark brown eyes—started to head in my direction, so I put on my instinctual fake smile as he came closer.

"Is this seat taken?"

An hour passed, but not in silence as you're probably expecting, because there's something about strangers: they're new. A clean slate. An escape from everything wrong in your own world, and a new one to immerse yourself in. But they always have this initial, unforgettable vibe, and it's either entirely encouraging or disapproving. Fortunately, for me, these worlds around me encouraged hope with their great character that appreciated every little thing about a person, flaws and all.

Time elapsed in joy and smiles while I was almost choking on my food due to laughter because there was nothing to be afraid of. I realized that the people here with me were freed in this seminar, not encaged like I thought. They weren't constrained by the reputation they had created in their home city but instead could create a new image while diving in the worlds of others around them, learning life stories, and having fun with new personalities with open perspectives about one's character—unlike the tainted lens looked through by their home folks. So I enjoyed myself. I was truly happy. And it felt great. I smiled a genuine smile as conversation flew with time, and I sat a bit taller to exude the comfort I found with these people instead of clamming up on myself and hunching into a ball.

I went to class with Seth after breakfast ended, and I found myself feeling more comfortable. When I started talking to the other teens, I noticed something. Some of the people who came here were the same age as the students in my grade and me, so what was the difference between the two groups that made one of them like me and the other hate me? After all, I was the same person. And that's when I figured it out. The dividing factor between the two groups was time.

The people in my grade have known me for about seven years now, if they went to elementary school with me, while the teens at the seminar knew me for seven *hours* after the first day was over. And I realized that in that time, you either make people hate you or love you, and the more time passes, the greater the chance that it could go either way. In school, I was too caught up with my anxiety in every little move I made that I didn't give enough reasons to the people in my class to like me, so they had no choice but to hate me, or at the very least, be unsure and scared of interacting with me.

But the teens in the class, I've given reasons for them to like me, being upbeat and sincere. And once I discerned this difference, I accepted it, hatred and all, because I realized this state wasn't permanent; I could still convince the people in my class there was a reason to be friends with me, even if it would be an uphill battle.

My friends left because they couldn't appreciate me, but that's their problem. Each person is rich in their own way; people just have more selective tastes than others, and it's entirely their fault for not being able to see beauty, ignoring it, or discounting it due to previous events (like most people did to me) in places that others are able to see it. And this enlightenment made me optimistic; there were five years left for me to change my image of loneliness, anxiety, and depression into something that I could keep my head up about and people would accept. It had to start with myself though, the only person who truly understands me. I had to accept and love myself before anyone else could, and that would take a while and some support which this seminar gave me.

The second day of the seminar passed by almost exactly like the first; a speaker came in to address the teen class, Allie discussed setting life goals and how to properly ask the adults at the seminar for their assistance in our goals when we sit with them at the meal tables, and the teens chattered away about TV shows, music, computer games, and dreams. The only thing that set the second day apart from the first day was the fact that we tried to host a movie night with *Mulan* that resulted in people falling asleep on each other, and I think that was when I knew how easy it was to tip this scale between love and hate, respect and degradation. It's easy to change how someone thinks of you only if you spend enough time that matters with them. Not the type of time that passes when you're in the same class with a person and discuss classwork once in a while. No, the type of time that matters is when you learn something about the other person. You learn you have the same interests, or watch the same TV shows, or do the same sport. That's the kind of time that matters. It's when you share, as cheesy as it sounds.

Now, when I'm on the edge of sleep, I think about how that wasn't the only thing that set the second day apart from the first. The teens and, to some extent, the adults at the seminar were so encouraging when we did activities with Allie. Their support was further exemplified through the practice of giving praise at the dinner table, when each person talked about their goals. This gave me hope in the human race. Not everyone is an unsupportive, narrow-minded piece of trash who can barely have the guts to stand by a person when they need it the most; some people are unafraid to accept difference and welcome everyone with open arms and sincere compassion. And it gave me hope to find someone like that, if this entire seminar was filled with those kinds of people. It was optimism about finding support and believing it was out there, something I haven't heard from myself in the longest time.

The third day was a bit more challenging, you could say. In fact, it was supposed to be so intense that Allie called it "Breakdown Day." I walked into the classroom with Seth again, talking about *Doctor Who* and all the relationships behind the sci-fi TV show. We walked into the familiar half-circle of seats again and took our usual spots near the end located at the right side of the room. Elena, who I met the day before in a group activity held by one of the instructors in the teen room, took the seat to the left of me and talked about some of her music interests that we shared while Seth got water from the back of the room.

The other teens started to stream in, and Allie finally took her seat at the front of the class before explaining what we were going to do today for the first half of the day. Like Allie said, another speaker came in to talk about the journey of being a lawyer and had a presentation for us to facilitate the process of taking notes, if we even wanted to. After finishing his lecture, the lawyer then held a Q&A for us to ensure there weren't any lingering questions the teens had that would go unanswered.

After the lawyer finished, break started and Seth, Elena, and I left to get muffins from the snack table. I got a water bottle, while Elena and Seth waited for coffee. After they got their cups of caffeine, we all walked back to the teen room. I didn't feel nervous of what was to come; I trusted that Allie wouldn't put us up to anything too daunting that she thought we couldn't handle.

I wish I could say something about what Allie had in store for the teens, but I can't (I signed a nondisclosure contract stating I couldn't discuss what was shared during that day's activity); all you need to know is that she taught us that pain isn't unique—its something everyone has in common. It's a sensation felt 'round the world. More likely than not, you'll find someone who understands your pain to some degree. Some degree of understanding is better than none at all. I used to think that because some people turn to drugs as an escape, instead of moping all day, it would prevent them from understanding my pain. No matter a person's skin tone, gender, or thought process, they feel pain, and there's someone who's going through the same thing and has climbed out of that same hole before. Not only that, but they will help you climb, and there's no shame in accepting help. That doesn't make you less of a person; it makes you *human*, so you shouldn't beat yourself up or discount your worth just because you took advantage of what you were offered. It makes you smart and proud for being able to climb at all instead of staying down there and digging yourself deeper.

The next two days were full of times I couldn't have fathomed in my previous life, with exuberant smiles, laughter, and hugs.

Elena and I talked more about all the TV shows that basically dictated our lives: *How to Get Away With Murder, Scandal, Stranger Things*, and more, while Seth got busy with a girl in the teen program. We all went down to the pool after Allie was done teaching at around 9:00 p.m., dipping our toes in the warm Jacuzzi and spontaneously singing a cappella radio hits horribly before sleeping.

But that's not all that happened. In the days that followed "Breakdown Day," I could feel this unbreakable bond in the air wherever the teens went. The sense of friendship and support was so profound you could smell it—or maybe that was Seth's cologne—nonetheless, it made me realize that this unbreakable camaraderie was what I wanted, and the fact that I could achieve it in approximately three days made me realize, despite the fact I've never felt this bond outside of this seminar, it wouldn't be impossible to achieve. So it enabled me to look forward to the new school year in order to create this sort of relationship of *you can tell me anything* with people I saw almost every day. Above all, though, it also let me see that there are people I can talk to who legitimately enjoy my company, and that if this room was filled with people who did, there must be at least one person back home who would.

So I shouldn't get down on myself if I hadn't gotten along with the people I had interacted with during my years in school.

Instead, I could remain hopeful, because hope is a beautiful thing. It shines a light in times of darkness, creates another world outside the box of ideas, and reminds you that the journey is not over, that it's never too late to change, and that happiness is out there waiting for you.

The last night of the seminar, we all had s'mores at the hotel fireplace. I hugged Elena goodbye at the end of our little party because she said I wasn't going to see her in the morning; her flight was at 5:00. A few other people left, and we all teared up a bit, but that's when I knew I had healed. I wasn't afraid of being invested in someone or the hurt that would eventually result from it; of pouring my love, time, and soul into someone other than myself; or of letting someone knock down my walls of "safety" that seemed more like an unnecessary precaution. But then I realized that these walls aren't unnecessary. You can't just let anyone and everyone into your life; otherwise, your life wouldn't be yours and personal wouldn't be personal—it'd be a public display for people to see at all times. However, these walls shouldn't prevent you from living life. The walls that protect a castle don't inhibit its residents from leaving; likewise, the walls of personal being shouldn't disable your ability to step outside of your comfort zone and get to know people in your class and let them get to know you, to be unafraid of asking for help instead of thinking it makes you look weak, to be yourself and be trusting. Walls weren't meant to prevent the king or queen from getting out; they were meant for protection when needed.

The seminar ended with a feeling that was bittersweet. I was excited to go back home so I could right my wrongs at school, but at the same time, I didn't want to leave. These teens were the first ones to make me feel appreciated. Cared about. Loved. These total strangers were able to uplift me and make me feel optimistic. Like I have a future. And I will never forget them because of that.

The trip back home was the same as it was coming to Nevada—passing the same desolate hills; bland, green signs; seemingly lifeless towns—but also different. There was something about returning home in the soothing shade of sunset that was immersive and special, like going back to a place where you knew the people like the back of your hand, but where you were still struck with the audacity of wonder. It was like looking through a glass pane at the cradling night sky and knowing everything would be all right.

Chapter 14

MONDAY, AUGUST 24, 2015

First day back at school. One of the only days my mom would always take me to school. No knife. No work. Well, at least not yet. But there was still zero period, and I really didn't want to know how things would turn out with Chris. My mom pulled the car up to the curb and put the car in park.

"Have fun," she said.

I waved goodbye in response and kept walking into the hallway while I heard her car drive away from the school.

Near the end of chamber choir, all of the sections were sight-reading a new piece Mr. Helinski had given us. The new counselor, Mr. Reld, walked into the choir room and watched us. Soon, the homeroom bell rang and the students streamed out, but Mr. Reld came over to me and asked if I would talk to him.

"Umm...I have to get to homeroom on time and I don't know where it is right now. Could we talk at snack break?" I asked Mr. Reld.

"Sure. Just remember to come to my office at snack break then."

Chapter 15

The counselor looked puzzled as he read the email response from one of my teachers. After a minute or so, he looked enlightened and turned back toward me.

"So, I was able to change your classes so you don't have to put up with anyone who has caused you trouble recently. That's basically all I can do. Just keep your head up, Michael. It might be weird at first, but I promise you that having new people in your class isn't that uncomfortable. And feel free to talk to me any time if you feel like there's anything wrong. Do you think going to therapy would help you?"

"I prefer not; I think I'm good for now."

"Well, if you don't want to talk to me when you do feel troubled, because we all do at some point in our lives, don't feel afraid to at least talk to a hotline; the National Suicide Prevention Lifeline can be contacted at 1-800-273-8255 in case you want to talk."

"Thank you." I said as I smiled. "May I go now? I'm a bit hungry and wanna get some chips," I said while chuckling faintly.

"Sure. Hope you like your classes."

"Thank you again," I said as I grabbed my backpack and hoisted it over my shoulder. I walked out of the office, excited for the new school year. This was a fresh start. This was a chance to change and to listen. Not to the denouncing comments of other people or the condescending voice in my head, but to the people who matter and care about me. Because there's always someone out there. And, yeah, it might be sad if that person right now is currently my counselor and not an actual student, but I know *someone's* always looking out for me. That's the only way to overcome sadness: constant awareness. You need to remember everyone is loved by someone and consistently hold onto that fact throughout your entire life with every breath and step you take. And that's what I planned to do—to remember I have a purpose and matter to someone.

I came home to see my mother sitting down at the table waiting for me. She jumped up and came up to me as I locked the door behind me.

"Welcome home, sweetie. What did the counselor say?"

"He changed my classes so I wouldn't have any problems, and I'd love to chat, Mom, but my math teacher gave me a ton of homework."

"Okay. Don't stress out too much. And remember. I love you."

I looked directly into my mother's eyes as I replied. "I love you too, Mom."

The National Suicide Prevention Lifeline
can be contacted at 1-800-273-8255

Did you know:

- Suicide is the second leading cause of death for ages 10-24.

- Suicide is the second leading cause of death for college-age youth and ages 12–18.

- More teenagers and young adults die from suicide than from cancer, heart disease, AIDS, birth defects, stroke, pneumonia, influenza, and chronic lung disease, combined.

- Each day in our nation, there are an average of over 3,470 attempts by young people grades 9–12. If these percentages are additionally applied to grades 7 and 8, the numbers would be higher.

- Four out of five teens who attempt suicide have given clear warning signs.

Facts courtesy of the Jason Foundation at
prp.jasonfoundation.com/facts/youth-suicide-statistics/

***

We want you to know that you make a difference in this world in some way, each and every day. This world would not be the same without you. Even on the day you think you're not seen, you most likely made a difference in someone's life. Every smile and every "hello" makes a difference.

We see you!

You make a difference.

Anti-Bullying Resources

Videos:

dontbullyonline.com/video

youtube.com/watch?v=A1J5IXV6P54

youtube.com/watch?v=OcgAF8GcBIw

greatschools.org/gk/articles/best-viral-antibullying-videos

Websites:

Teens Against Bullying:
pacerteensagainstbullying.org

Real Teens Speak Out:
pacerteensagainstbullying.org/you-are-not-alone/real-teens-
speak-out

Teen Essay about bullying:
teenink.com/hot_topics/bullying/article/454500/Stand-Up

Other teen books about bullying:
communitylibrary.net/drupal7/content/teen-books-about-
dealing-bullying

Teach Anti Bullying is a non-profit organization Founded by Dr. Claudio V. Cerullo in 2011 to assist the victims of bullying. Dr. Cerullo endorsed this book, *Fade Away*.
teachantibullying.com

Poems about bullying:
nobullying.com/poems-about-bullying

53740352R00057

Made in the USA
San Bernardino, CA
26 September 2017